THE PAINTER
WHO LOVED CHICKENS

To B—*the* woman in my life

The text of this book is set in 16 pt. Cochin. The gouache paintings are
rendered on 140 lb. hot-press Fabriano and Canson Mi-Tientes.

Copyright © 1995 by Olivier Dunrea
All rights reserved
Published simultaneously in Canada by HarperCollins*CanadaLtd*
Color separations by Hong Kong Scanner Craft
Printed in the United States of America by Berryville Graphics
First edition, 1995

Library of Congress Cataloging-in-Publication Data
Dunrea, Olivier.
The painter who loved chickens / by Olivier Dunrea. — 1st ed.
p.   cm.
[1. Artists—Fiction.   2. Chickens—Fiction.]   I. Title.
PZ7.D922Pai   1995b   [E]—dc20   94-27562   CIP   AC

THE PAINTER
WHO LOVED CHICKENS

OLIVIER DUNREA

Farrar · Straus · Giroux

New York

BROWN LEGHORN

There once lived a man who loved chickens—very much. He made his home in the city, but he dreamed of living on a farm. And on his farm he would have chickens, lots of chickens.

The man worked as a painter. He painted pictures of people, poodles, and penguins. Many people bought these pictures. But what the man really wanted to paint was chickens. No one wanted pictures of chickens.

BARRED ROCK

Every morning the man ate his breakfast and listened to the radio. He drank strong coffee with cream. He read the newspaper. Then he went into his studio and painted. He painted all day, without stopping for lunch. The pictures he painted took a long time, and there was often a list of people waiting to buy them.

GOLDEN CAMPINE

Whenever he could spare a minute from these paintings, the man drew and painted pictures of chickens. He painted black chickens. He painted big chickens. He painted speckled hens. He painted crowing roosters. His pictures of chickens made him happy.

By painting pictures all day long, the man earned enough money to live. But he could never earn enough to buy a farm. He did not want a large farm, just one large enough for himself and his chickens.

BLACK MINORCA

One day a man with a black mustache came to his studio. "I want to buy a picture," he said gruffly.

The painter stopped reading and looked at the man.

"I'm sorry," he said, "but I have no pictures ready to sell at the moment. Perhaps if you come back in a week or so."

"Come back in a week!" shouted the man. "I want a picture *now*. If I can't get it here, I'll get it somewhere else."

"I *am* sorry," said the painter.

The man snorted, turned on his heel, and stomped out the door.

The painter sighed and continued painting. Would he ever find someone who really appreciated his work?

WHITE GIANT

The painter painted and painted. Months passed. He became more and more unhappy in the city, and he longed more and more for a farm. He stared at the rain outside the window. It was a cheerless, heartless city rain.

The painter looked at his blank paper. He could not paint another person. He could not paint another poodle. He could not paint another penguin. But since he needed money, he could not paint chickens.

BLACK LANGSHAN

The painter sighed and picked up his paintbrush. Without thinking, he painted a simple shape in the center of the paper. He gazed at the shape and smiled. It was an egg!

Just then, a well-dressed woman entered the studio.

"Hello," said the woman.

"Hello," replied the painter. "May I help you?"

"Yes," said the woman, smiling. "I would like to see your pictures."

"Certainly. I happen to have quite a few at the moment."

SILKIE

The painter took out a portfolio and showed her his pictures of people. The woman shook her head. He showed her his pictures of poodles. Again the woman shook her head. The painter showed her his pictures of penguins.

The woman sighed. "I'm sorry," she said. "I was hoping to see something different."

Then the woman noticed the painting of the egg. She picked up the sheet of paper and looked hard at the picture. "This is what I'm looking for!" the woman cried.

BLUE COCHIN

"I'm afraid that's not for sale," said the painter quietly. "I've never painted a picture quite like that before."

"Oh, but I must have it!" exclaimed the woman.

"But—" began the painter, "but—it's only an egg."

"But it's beautiful!" cried the woman. "I'll buy all the eggs you can paint."

The woman opened her purse and took out her checkbook. She wrote out a check to the painter and handed it to him. It was for an enormous amount of money.

The painter began to protest. "I'm sorry, madam," he said, stammering. "But this is far too much money to pay for a picture of an egg."

NEW HAMPSHIRE RED

"You don't understand," said the woman. "I have been looking for a picture just like this for a long time, a very long time. There's something magical about this picture—its composition, its color—it's lovely!"

The man could not believe his ears. "If you would wait just a moment," he said to the woman, "I have some more paintings you may find interesting."

The painter pulled open a drawer and took out a battered cardboard portfolio. He carefully untied the ribbons and opened the portfolio. Inside were his drawings and paintings of chickens.

WHITE-CRESTED BLACK POLISH

The woman smiled. "You drew and painted all these chickens?"

"Yes," said the painter. "I made them for myself. I didn't think anyone would want pictures of chickens."

The woman looked through all the pictures in the portfolio. She picked up each one and studied it. Finally she laid down the last picture. She sat and stared at the paintings. Her eyes sparkled.

"I want to buy them all," she said to the painter. "I think they are wonderful and should be seen by everybody. I must have them."

The painter was speechless. How could he sell the pictures of his beloved chickens?

LIGHT BRAHMA

The woman broke into his thoughts. "I know I am asking a great deal," she said. "I can see that you *do* love chickens. You don't belong in the city. You should live on a farm and surround yourself with real chickens. With the money I'll give you for these paintings, you could buy a farm. A really nice farm."

The painter nodded slowly. "Yes," he said at last. "I will sell you the pictures. But I would like to keep just one."

The painter and the woman agreed on a price for the pictures. Both were very pleased.

SILVER-GRAY DORKING

The painter bought a small farm with ancient stone buildings. And he bought a box of newly hatched chicks.

In the autumn the woman held an exhibition of the pictures of chickens. It was a tremendous success. Everyone came to see the marvelous pictures. The art critics said the paintings were the most spectacular ever made of farmyard fowl.

PARTRIDGE ROCK

On his farm the painter lovingly raised his brood of chicks, which grew into fine chickens. Some were speckled, with feathered feet. Some were small and brightly colored. Some were large and gray. Some were barred. Some were red. The entire flock was remarkable!

BUFF ORPINGTON

The woman visited the painter often. She fed the chickens and listened to their boisterous clucking. She always left the farm with a portfolio of new paintings of chickens—and a basketful of eggs!

Every autumn the woman exhibited the painter's latest paintings of chickens and eggs. The painter became famous. And he never again painted anything that he did not love to paint.